# Amazing Animals:
# Animals in Danger

# Amazing Animals: Animals in Danger

Peter Hepplewhite and Neil Tonge

Illustrated by
Robin Lawrie

MACMILLAN CHILDREN'S BOOKS

First published 2000
by Macmillan Children's Books
a division of Macmillan Publishers Ltd
25 Eccleston Place, London SW1W 9NF
Basingstoke and Oxford

www.macmillan.co.uk

Associated companies throughout the world

ISBN 0 330 39338 3

Copyright © Peter Hepplewhite and Neil Tonge 2000
Illustrations copyright © Robin Lawrie 2000

The right of Peter Hepplewhite and Neil Tonge to be identified as the
authors of this book has been asserted by them in accordance
with the Copyright, Designs and Patents Act 1988.

1 3 5 7 9 8 6 4 2

A CIP catalogue record for this book is available from the British Library.

Printed by Mackays of Chatham plc, Chatham, Kent.

# Contents

# Introduction

**A**nimals in Danger brings you some utterly amazing tales of brave beasts. Dare you share the thrills and spills of these four-legged and finned friends? Can they survive wars, hunters and murderers across 2,500 years of troubled times?

In ancient Macedonia, Bucephalus – the mighty black stallion – was frightened of his own shadow. He was rescued from his plight by an unhappy boy – who grew up to be Alexander the Great. Together they became an unbeatable team.

In medieval France a greyhound was witness to his master's murder. No problem – but then he set out to seek revenge against the killer, one of the king's bodyguards.

In the early 1800s Mocha Dick, the giant white whale, was ruler of the South Pacific – until whale hunters made him their number one target. By the 1970s whaling was banned but pirates don't obey laws. They hunted every whale in the sea, even those on the brink of extinction. Sometimes however, their victims hit back.

In 1868, Comanche, the wild mustang, was captured and trained as a mount for the 7th Cavalry in the American West. Eight years later he was amongst the troops marching with General Custer along the Little Big Horn River. Had his luck run out?

In 1881, in South Africa, a disabled railwayman, Jack Wild, rescued a young baboon from a market. The ape became the best friend he ever had.

In Victorian England, Lockhart's performing elephants were stars of the stage and the circus ring. Great, when they tamely showed their tricks. However, as you'll find out, they had some very bad habits.

In 1998 in Malmesbury, England, two pigs made their escape from the slaughterhouse and became world news – but can you blame them for trying to save their bacon?

# Alexander and Bucephalus

*Alexander the Great was born in 356BC and died in 323BC. In his short life he conquered an empire that stretched from Greece to India. Even today, he is remembered as one of the greatest leaders of all time. For nearly twenty years, through many deadly battles, his bravest friend was Bucephalus, the black stallion.*

## Family Problems

What do you do if your parents argue? Keep out of the way and don't take sides? Very wise. Young Alexander was never given that choice. He was a pawn in the angry war between his mother and father. Until the day he met Bucephalus – the day a frightened horse earned him the respect of his father.

That morning, King Philip of Macedonia stood outside the royal stables, his twelve-year-old son Alexander by his side. Although it was still early morning, the summer heat drummed on the parade ground and sweat trickled down Philip's broad forehead. The king, and it seemed half the court, were waiting for the stable-hands to bring out the new stallion. Demaratus, his close friend, had bought him the horse as a present and this was his first chance to inspect it. As he waited Philip looked at Alexander and frowned.

'Alexander is always edgy,' he thought. 'Never trusts me. His mother must have been telling him more nonsense. Perhaps this is one thing we can share – he's got a good eye for a horse.'

Alexander's home life was a battleground. Philip had regretted his marriage to the boy's mother, Olympias, almost from the beginning. He had met her on the island of Samothrace and fallen in love with her at first glance. To the young king she had seemed perfect. Good looking, raven-haired, and an unexpected bonus – a princess. Unhappily, their whirlwind romance soon fizzled out. After their marriage and the birth of Alexander the royal couple began to quarrel bitterly.

By the time he was five Alexander had been taught to hate his father. His early years had been filled with the sound of his parents bickering and brawling. After every argument, Olympias turned to her son for comfort. She cuddled Alexander fiercely, telling him the same daunting secret again and again.

'Don't worry, he isn't your real father. Your

fate was made in heaven. You are the son of a god. The world will fall at your feet.'

Olympias wasn't crazy. She worshipped ancient and powerful gods and saw visions. Her son, the gods told her, was divine and would blaze a trail across the world, like a shooting star. His achievements would far outshine those of his father, her despised husband.

Yet Philip did little to help his bewildered son. He was a hardened warrior and a skilled general. If his kingdom was threatened he attacked first, and usually won. He resented the proud wife that he could not control and her influence over Alexander. Although he loved the lad, Philip rarely showed it. When he might have won his son's devotion with a little praise, he was more likely to make fun of him.

In the buzzing excitement of the stable yard, Alexander saw his father's frown and took it as more disapproval. 'Will I ever be able to make him like me? Will he always hate me because of my mother,' he thought. Father and son should have spoken a kind word but both were stubborn and kept silent. In a few seconds the chance to talk was lost as Demaratus strode across the yard and slapped Philip on the back.

# *A Flawed Gift*

Demaratus and Philip went back a long way. His loyalty was unquestioned and he spoke to the king almost as an equal.

'Wait till you see him, Philip. I got him from that Thessalonian breeder I told you about. He cost me thirteen talents, but he's worth it.'

Philip smiled, thirteen talents was a fortune.

From anyone else such an extravagant present would have been suspicious. Courtiers often tried to buy favours, but with Demaratus he could relax.

'Thirteen talents,' the king joked, 'he's seen you coming. I could equip a troop of cavalry for that. What's he called? Demaratus' Folly?'

Demaratus pulled a hurt face and continued, 'You're as mean as an old woman haggling for eggs in a market. To bargain for a horse like this would have been a crime. Wait till you see him. Twelve years old. Mature, fierce and strong. A horse for a king, with a name to match. Bucephalus.'

'It means Ox Head,' Alexander murmured to himself. 'I wonder if he's as steady as an ox when a bear charges? Or will he spill my father over his head into the dust?'

Like all Macedonians, the boy lived to hunt. In his rugged kingdom bears and lions roamed the highlands and herds of deer were plentiful. Every Macedonian king had to be a good hunter to impress his people. Alexander knew a fine horse would help Philip keep his reputation as one of the bravest.

A clopping of hooves on the sun-baked parade ground announced the arrival of Bucephalus. But at first glance, father and son saw that there was a problem. The horse was certainly magnificent, but he was jittery. He seemed almost wild, not the calm and powerful stallion Demaratus had boasted of.

Bucephalus pulled at the reins and reared, as if he was terrified of the watching crowd. His hooves cut a deadly arc through the air and sent the stable hands ducking and diving. Gingerly one of them tried to mount him. But before he could get a tight grip with his knees, the horse hurled him onto the unforgiving dirt. And then tried to stomp on him for good measure. All attempts to soothe Bucephalus failed and soon two more riders tasted the dust.

'What's this, Demaratus?' demanded Philip, at first more amused than angry. 'A gift or an assassination attempt? That Thessalonian dealer will be hiding in Athens, showing your talents to the dancing girls and telling stories about the mad horse he sold to a Macedonian fool.'

But Philip's joke had a serious point. It seemed Bucephalus was worthless. Riders sat bareback or on a simple cloth. Control came from the bit and the knees. A horse had to be steady and willing to please, or it was a danger.

## A Horse to Heal Wounds

'Take the useless brute away,' said the king, suddenly turning serious. It was a warning sign.

Philip's bad temper was renowned and the courtiers grew still. As Demaratus began to splutter an answer, Alexander eyed his father defiantly and spoke up.

'Sire, I think I know what the problem is. Let me try to ride him.'

At once the old anger boiled between them. Philip glared back. How dare the boy challenge his decision in front of everyone? And what if the young fool was injured? He was a good rider but not that good.

The king turned on his brash son, 'Boy, do you boast greater knowledge than your elders and betters? Do you think you are more skilled in horsemanship than they are?'

Alexander snapped back, 'I can manage that horse better than they do.'

'So what penalty will you pay for your rashness, if you fail?' challenged Philip.

'The price of the horse, Sire,' retorted Alexander.

At this Philip roared with laughter. He had to admit his son had fire in his belly.

'Come on then, Alexander, test your skills. If you succeed he's yours,' he said almost kindly.

Turning to the stablehands he yelled, 'Let the insolent boy try.' Uneasily they moved aside and handed over the halter. Who would the king blame, they worried, if the lad cracked his skull?

Alexander stroked Bucephalus' sweating neck and whispered gently in his ear. He had noticed one crucial factor that the men had missed – the highly strung animal was shying at his own shadow. Quietly Alexander turned the stallion towards the sun and as they moved Bucephalus began to calm down. The terrifying black apparition that had danced around him had gone.

Patting and smoothing his glistening coat, Alexander walked the horse around the parade ground. Murmuring praises, the boy chose his moment and leapt astride the stallion's back. Amid a stunned silence he cantered Bucephalus out of the yard and into open ground. Free from the buildings, boy and horse surged into a gallop. As they tore across the ground Alexander felt a sense of freedom he had rarely known before. This animal trusted him. It was open and honest, without tricks or mind games. It was the start of a friendship that lasted twenty years.

At first Philip and the onlookers were dumbstruck, then they burst into a chorus of yells.

'My son,' cried the king with tears of joy. 'Macedonia isn't big enough for you. You'll make it greater yet.'

★

Philip kept his promise and gave the troublesome horse to Alexander. He had finally seen that the boy deserved respect, and for a time they warmed to one another. When he was fifteen, the king trusted Alexander enough to leave him in charge of the country while he went to war. But it was a lull in a storm. When his father married another, younger, woman Alexander stormed out of the wedding feast. He was so angry at the insult to his mother that he became a rebel, hiding in the hills from royal troops sent to hunt him down. Some historians think he was even involved in Philip's murder in 336BC.

Three years after he became King of Macedonia himself, Alexander attacked the vast Persian Empire. He was mounted on Bucephalus as he led his armies across the Hellespont (the straits between Europe and Asia). For the next ten blood-soaked years he was unstoppable. In four great battles Alexander overthrew Darius, the fabled King of Kings, and with Persia firmly in his grasp moved on to India. Time and again he smashed armies far larger his own. And, as if fulfilling his mother's prophecy, he was hailed as a god by those he had defeated.

# Bucephalus –
# Headline History of a Legend

Ancient writers such as Plutarch and Arrian tell us Alexander's gripping story but don't give many details about Bucephalus. It was almost as if they took his reputation for granted. Even so, the incidents that can be pieced together have made him the most famous war horse in history. If there had been newspapers and TV reporters with Alexander's armies, Bucephalus would have made the headlines.

## Bucephalus Beats the Persians at their Own Game

Alexander taught Bucephalus to kneel in full harness. This meant he could mount the stallion easily while he was wearing armour. It was a trick he borrowed from the Persians.

## Only One Master

The gallant horse only allowed Alexander to ride him, anyone else who tried was thrown off. When the fighting was most dangerous Bucephalus was as deadly as his master. He lashed

out with his hooves — and one blow was enough
to break a bone or split a skull.

## Bucephalus the Battle Winner

Alexander rode Bucephalus in every great
victory (except the battle of Granicus, when he
was lame) and the mighty horse saved his life a
dozen times. The sight of Alexander on his fiery
stallion inspired his own men and put dread in
the souls of the enemy. Under Alexander's
leadership the Macedonian cavalry became a
war-winning force.

## Old Warriors Know Best

Although he seemed invincible, Bucephalus was a veteran, already 23, when the war with Persia began. Alexander knew that his friend was getting old and used a string of other horses to save his strength. When the army was on the march or he was inspecting troops, humdrum jobs, he rode other animals. But when action called, Alexander always sent for Bucephalus, his first charger.

## Kidnap Horror

In Hyrcania, near the Caspian Sea, the Macedonians launched an attack against the Mardians. The Mardians lived in dense mountain forests and hit back with pinprick raids. On one of these, the unthinkable happened: a party of squires in charge of the royal horses was ambushed and Bucephalus was captured.

## Bring Bucephalus Back – or Else

The raiders didn't realize who they had kidnapped and Alexander was frantic in case Bucephalus was sold to a farmer or trader.

Nothing could be worse, the proud stallion ending his days as a broken-down packhorse on some backwoods farm. Alexander sent out heralds with a blunt message: 'Bring Bucephalus back within a few days or I will wipe out your people – man, woman and child.' As he expected his friend was returned safely – with humble apologies.

## Brave Bucephalus Fights Last Battle

The old horse went to war for the last time in 327BC, when he was over 30. The Indian king, Porus, had decided to stop Alexander at the River Jhelum in the Punjab. His army was five times bigger and included 200 war elephants. In the opening moves of the battle Alexander fought a skirmish with Indian chariots and Bucephalus was wounded – hit by spear thrusts in the neck and flanks. Struggling against the pain, he carried his master away from the fighting before he collapsed. Fearing the worst but unable to stay with his friend, Alexander switched horses and fought on. But, when the grim battle ended in victory, he felt no joy. Bucephalus had died of his injuries.

# Fabulous Lost Tomb

Broken-hearted, Alexander led the funeral procession for the old war horse. The brave beast was buried in a tomb in the centre of a new city, called Bucephala, in his honour. Sadly the site was not well chosen. Bucephala was founded on the west bank of the River Jhelum, an untamed river that regularly changed course. Soon the area was washed by floods and the site of the tomb lost for ever. However, modern archaeologists still live in hope of finding it. What flood waters have hidden, they might one day, uncover.

# Alive in Legend

In Persia, modern-day Iran, the legend of Sikander (Alexander) has been passed down for over two thousand years. Since this is a Persian legend it claims that Sikander was really the son of the Great King, Darius. As time passed his adventures became ever more fabulous. One episode tells that he rescued Egypt from the black and deadly Zangs – an invading army of monsters that sucked the blood and ate the brains of their victims. Of course, when Sikander rode into battle, his horse was as awesome as himself – a jet black, bull-horned stallion.

## Battle Elephant

What's an elephant doing in a chapter about a heroic horse? Well, some historians claim there was another animal, as courageous as Bucephalus, at the battle of Jhelum. The leader of the Indian army, King Porus, rode to war on a giant elephant. Sadly the chronicles of the time don't name Porus' mount, only commenting that it was 'of the very largest size' and so was probably a male.

During the fighting the great beast valiantly protected his master, trampling men underfoot or hurling them aside with his trunk. He was clever too, and picked his ground carefully, not allowing Macedonian spearmen to get behind him and attack his vunerable flanks. Yet even the best efforts of the elephant couldn't save Porus from several cruel wounds. Sensing that his rider was badly injured, he carried him from the battlefield, knelt so that the king could dismount and tenderly pulled a spear from his body.

Is this believable? Or could it be that the Indians had heard the legend of Bucephalus, and decided that they too needed an animal hero?

# The Avenging Dog

## A Howl in the Night

*Most dog owners like to think their pet is clever and well trained. But does canine intelligence go beyond learning a few tricks? Could a dog have a sense of justice? If a faithful hound witnessed the brutal murder of its master, could it seek revenge? There's no doubt about it, according to this French legend from the Middle Ages.*

Sieur de Narsac stirred in his bed. Something had woken him and he wasn't pleased.

*Scratch . . . scratch . . . yeooowl . . . scratch . . . scratch . . .*

'Paris, rowdy Paris. Braying horses and braying people late into the night – and now this,' he moaned. De Narsac hated staying in the family town house and longed to be back in the quiet Breton countryside.

*Scratch . . . scratch . . . scratch . . . yeooowl . . . scratch . . . scratch . . . yeooowl . . .*

'Go away,' he groaned and pulled the feather pillow over his head, but there it was again.

*Scratch . . . scratch . . . scratch . . . scratch . . . yeooowl . . . scratch . . . scratch . . . yeooooowl . . .*

What had happened to the servants? How could they sleep through this infernal row? 'Merciful God in Heaven, someone will feel the toe of my boot,' he mumbled as he staggered reluctantly from between the warm blankets.

*Scratch . . . scratch . . . scratch . . . yeooowl . . . scratch . . . scratch . . . yeooooowl . . .*

The noise came more urgently, like the sound of a dog desperate to escape from a trap. It had to be coming from outside, a neighbour's animal. He would have a few choice words to say in the morning.

Stamping through the hall, he flung open the door and jumped back in alarm. Lying across the doorway was a huge, gaunt greyhound. The dog's ribs stood out like the bars of a gridiron under its smooth coat. Its tongue lolled out of open, gasping jaws. Its eyes were bloodshot and its limbs shook. The poor beast was exhausted and starving – as if at the end of a nightmare journey.

As de Narsac peered out the dog struggled to stand up and thrust its nose into the startled man's hand.

'What is it, boy?' he said gently. 'What are you doing here? Are you lost? Hang on . . . don't I know you . . . ? You're Aubrey's favourite dog . . . What's the matter? What's happened . . . eh, boy?'

De Narsac began to feel uneasy. He hadn't seen his friend Aubrey de Montdidier for over a week now. Aubrey had missed Mass at the Church of Our Lady on Sunday, but there was nothing unusual in that. He loved his bed even more than de Narsac did. But he had also missed the tournament at Saint Katherine's. Now that was strange. Aubrey enjoyed the thrill of the tilt and had arranged to meet de Narsac and other young nobles there. They had planned to make a day of it: plenty of red wine, watch some good fights and chase a few servant girls. When Aubrey had failed to turn up the others had asked around, but no one had been worried . . . until now!

De Narsac woke the kitchen boy and ordered him to bring food for the greyhound. He watched intently as it wolfed down every scrap. It was clear the dog had not eaten for days. The mystery deepened. Aubrey looked after his dogs better than his servants. Why should this one be so neglected unless . . . unless what?

No sooner had the greyhound finished than it slunk into a corner and collapsed into a deep sleep. Yawning, de Narsac returned to his bed, but rest would not come. Tomorrow, he decided, he would search Paris for his friend. He tossed and turned restlessly, then as the sky became tinged with pink dawn light, he heard the scuffle

of paws. Aubrey's hound walked over to him and pulled at his sleeve. He whined and grumbled as the dog almost yanked him out of bed. Clearly it wanted de Narsac to follow him. Now!

## *Murder*

Desperately the greyhound paced the room while he dressed. As soon as he was ready the dog led him to the door and out into the quiet streets.

'Not even time for breakfast, boy?' he asked sadly, thinking of his empty stomach. 'What trouble has Aubrey got himself into? Beaten up by money lenders or locked up by the angry father of some girl?'

Looking back to check that the man was always in sight, the dog trotted through the narrow, twisting streets of the city. To de Narsac's surprise they headed across town and out through the protecting walls by the Porte (Gate) St Martin. Once in the open country they turned towards the Forest of Bondy. De Narsac grimaced – the forest was infested with outlaws. He checked that his sword was in easy reach and ran smoothly in its scabbard. If there was trouble he was ready.

In the woodland, a narrow path ran through dark glades, each one a perfect site for an ambush. As they wound their way deeper in, De Narsac's sense of dread grew. He was sure that

someone was watching and glanced nervously at
the undergrowth. Suddenly in the gloom of a
dense grove, the dog began to growl and
whimper. Tugging at de Narsac's cloak it led him
to a mound of freshly dug earth under a giant
oak. It looked like a grave.

Fearing the worst, de Narsac set off back to
Paris to get help. But he could not persuade the
dog to come with him. The greyhound lay
stretched on the newly turned soil, whining
piteously. When he returned several hours later,

with a magistrate and a work gang, the dog hadn't moved. A few minutes' work with broad spades confirmed the worst. As the damp earth was cleared, the body of Aubrey de Montdidier was exposed to the horrified gaze of his friend. Dried blood from stab wounds still crusted his fine clothes. Aubrey had been murdered!

The men built a litter of tree boughs and carried their tragic load back to Paris. Soon after, Aubrey was reburied in a Christian grave, his grief-stricken relatives standing forlornly by. The magistrate investigated but no one had come forward with any evidence – except the faithful dog. The murder remained a riddle.

Now de Narsac had a new companion. The greyhound had followed Aubrey's corpse home and from then on, rarely left de Narsac's side. It slept at the foot of his bed, ate from his table and walked at his heels when he left the house. It was as if the dog was protecting its new master from the harm that had cruelly snatched away the old.

## Suspicion

A few weeks later, the two were threading their way through the crowded Rue St Martin. Coming towards them were a group of the king's bodyguard, their smart uniforms drawing admiring glances from passers-by. De Narsac waved, he knew a few of them well. He and Aubrey had spent more than a few wild nights in their company.

Suddenly de Narsac was startled by a savage growl from the greyhound. Shocked, he looked down. The dog was the best trained he had ever known. What was the matter? Then, to his horror, it attacked. Hackles raised, and snarling wildly, it sprang for the throat of one of the king's men, Chevalier Macaire. (A chevalier is a French knight.) Macaire was caught off balance and was only saved by the other knights, who beat away the dog with their walking sticks.

De Narsac apologized, 'I'm so sorry. I've never seen him behave like this. I don't know what's come over him.'

Seizing the greyhound by the scruff of the neck, he hauled it away.

As they retreated down the street the dog thrashed from side to side, desperate to renew the assault. De Narsac's first reaction was anger – the animal had made a fool of him in front of the others. He yanked it away roughly, then a second, uneasy feeling came over him. Aubrey and Macaire had never liked each other. He had heard rumours that they had come to blows more than once. Was there a link?

'No,' he said to himself. 'Don't be stupid . . .'

★

A week later de Narsac and Macaire passed in the royal park and again the greyhound went berserk. As before, Macaire was only saved from its tearing jaws by his companions. This time, however, de Narsac watched the chevalier closely.

'Keep that damned dog on a short lead or next time I'll kill it,' the knight swore.

But he looked unsure, like a blustering bully finally tackled by someone his own size.

Stories of the greyhound and Macaire raced through the court and reached the ears of the king. He too had heard whisperings of a violent quarrel between the chevalier and de Montdidier. Now Aubrey's old dog bitterly hated the young officer in his guard. Was this a clue to the murder? He decided to investigate.

Early one morning de Narsac was amazed to find himself summoned to the court. His family was noble, but hardly had the ear of the king. The messenger, however, was clear: 'Be sure to bring Aubrey de Montdidier's dog. His Majesty is most eager to see it.'

Following closely at his master's heels, the greyhound trotted into the royal audience chamber at the Hotel St–Pol. Ahead of them was the king, surrounded by his courtiers and bodyguard. As de Narsac bowed low, the dog let out a short snarl of fury. It had spotted Macaire and before anyone could react, sprang to the attack. Astonished courtiers screamed, yelled and jumped aside as the hound closed in on its prey. For several minutes the court was in chaos until the dog was tied up.

## Trial by Combat

De Narsac groaned. He feared the king would have the 'mad' dog put down and banish him from Paris. But his fears were groundless. The king was fascinated. There was a mystery here he was determined to solve. He felt sure that Chevalier Macaire had something to answer for. The judgement of God would decide.

'Let there be trial by combat,' he ordered. 'A fight to the death, this very afternoon, between the accused – the man, and the accuser – the dog.'

The site chosen for the combat was a piece of waste ground often used for duels. News that this fight was different had spread quickly and a huge crowd gathered. The chevalier was armed with a short stick, thick and strong. The dog was given an empty barrel to hide in if it needed time to recover.

When the king gave the signal – a flick of his

wrist – de Narsac released the greyhound. The combat had begun. De Narsac felt helpless. What hope did a dog have against a highly trained knight? He believed Macaire would beat his pet to death with a few well-aimed blows. But the dog seemed to understand that it had been given a chance to seek revenge. Snarling, bounding, barking, leaping, always on the move, it circled Macaire. The chevalier took aim and lashed out with his stick, but time and again he hit the air.

Soon his breath came in short, troubled gasps and his blows became clumsier still. His friends in the bodyguard were stunned. Macaire was a skilled warrior. What was wrong with him?

The dog too was tiring, but fought on like a hell hound. This was the man who had killed his master – he had to die. Hurtling like a rock from a catapult, the greyhound dodged under the stick and fastened his teeth at Macaire's throat. The chevalier screamed and tore at the dog's jaws with his hands.

'Help me. Get him off,' Macaire yelled. 'I did it. I killed Montdidier. Just help me.'

The greyhound was pulled away but Macaire was not spared for long. The king commanded that he be taken away and executed – after he had seen a priest and confessed his sins. And the dog? The king told de Narsac to keep it and treat such a faithful hound well. It was an order that he was happy to obey.

# Comanche, Survivor of Little Big Horn

## The Retired Hero

Fort Abraham Lincoln, Dakota Territory, 1878. Colonel Samuel D. Sturgis, commanding officer of the Seventh United States' Cavalry, looked out of his office window and groaned. His neat lawns were covered in horse droppings and his prize sunflowers were headless stalks. Comanche had been raiding – again!

Lieutenant E. A. Garlington, his Adjutant, glanced over the Colonel's shoulder and grinned. 'Well, you did give him the freedom of the fort, sir, so he's only following your orders. Like a good soldier,' he joked.

'Sometimes I think we should sell him to one of these wild west shows that keep pestering us,' the Colonel smiled back. 'The men are already calling him the Second Commanding Officer of the Seventh. He'll be sitting at my desk next, stamping three months' leave for the entire regiment with his hoof print. Come to think of it, Lieutenant, he's such a hero Washington would probably approve.'

As the two men watched, Comanche clopped slowly into view, still limping from his wounds. 'I still don't understand how he survived,' mused Sturgis. '263 men and 319 horses wiped out at Little Big Horn because of that fool Custer, and this old boy came through it . . . just. What a story, Lieutenant. I can still hardly believe it myself. If only he could talk . . .'

## Native American Wars

In the 1870s small and bitter wars with Native Americans flared like forest fires across the American West. The US army played a deadly game of hide and seek with some of the best horsemen in the world: the plains Indians. The battleground was huge, 6½ million square kilometres, from the Mississippi River to the Pacific Ocean.

The Native American tribes (Sioux, Kiowa, Crow, Apache, Cheyenne and others) had learned the tricks of the white men the hard way – through broken treaties and stolen territory. Now they fought back, ruthlessly attacking the rising tide of miners, ranchers and farmers invading their ancient lands. Great warriors such

as Sitting Bull, Crazy Horse and Cochise scored a string of victories.

To face them, ten tough regiments of US Cavalry were scattered in lonely forts across the American West. The troopers were as mixed as the migrants pouring into the United States. Irish brogue was as common in the ranks as American twang, while Italian and German accents also featured strongly.

Mounted patrols could last months, as they vainly chased Native American war bands across hundreds of miles of harsh terrain. And the climate was as cruel as the enemy. In winter the High Plains were hit by Arctic-like snow storms with temperatures often plunging below −20°C. In summer, the sun scoured the southern deserts. No wonder a forlorn troopers' song began:

*Forty miles a day on beans and hay in the regular Army O!*

## Cavalry Horse

Comanche's army career began in 1868. He was one of many wild mustangs captured by horse hunters and sold to the US army. In June that year, he was among a bunch of 40 remounts taken to Fort Leavenworth, Kansas. As the horses milled uneasily about their corral, Comanche caught the eye of Captain Keogh.

Keogh was a rugged Irishman who loved a scrap. As a soldier of fortune he had fought for the Pope in Italy, before crossing to the USA to seek more thrills in the American Civil War. When that ended the thought of peace was too much for him to bear and he joined the newly formed Seventh Cavalry, led by General George Armstrong Custer. Soon he was in charge of 'I' Troop.

Keogh understood horses and picked out a six-year-old bay as the best of the rookie recruits. The mustang was 15 hands, with a small white star on his forehead and a white near-hind fetlock. Cavalrymen were expected to buy their own horses and the Captain paid over the regulation price, $90. He soon knew it was money well spent. The horse had an easy stride, a patient nature and showed great stamina on long and hard patrols.

Keogh's new mount earned his name in his first fight — a skirmish with a band of Comanches at Bluff Creek, Kansas. There are two versions of this story, and both may be right.

## How to Name a War Horse

**Version One:**

Tells us that, as the Indians closed in, the mustang was hit by an arrow in his right hindquarter. Shocked and hurt, he screamed out loud. The piercing sound was just like the war cry of the attacking Indians, so troopers nearby christened him Comanche.

**Version Two:**

Agrees that the horse was injured but goes on to say that he still carried his rider for the rest of the fight — even though the broken shaft of the arrow was sticking out of the wound. Back in camp he stood still and calm while the farrier took out the steel head. After this, Keogh called him Comanche because he was as brave as the enemy he had just met in battle.

## Little Big Horn

On 25 June 1876 General Custer led the Seventh Cavalry against a Native American encampment on the Little Big Horn River. Custer, nicknamed Long Hair by the Indians, believed he was attacking an easy target — in fact he had blundered into a force of 3,000 warriors eager for a fight. None of Custer's men lived to tell the tale, but many Native Americans did.

Kill Eagle, a Sioux chief explained: 'We hit them like a hurricane, like bees swarming out of a hive.'

Crow King watched the Bluecoats dismount to fight: 'They tried to hold onto their horses, but as we pressed them closer they let them go. We crowded them toward our main camp and killed them all. They kept in order and fought like brave warriors as long as they had a man left.'

Red Horse was more scathing: 'These soldiers became foolish, many throwing away their guns and raising their hands, saying, "Sioux, pity us, take us prisoners." The Sioux did not take a single soldier prisoner but killed them all; none were alive for even a few minutes.'

Sitting Bull remembered the end of the battle: 'Where the last stand was made, Long Hair stood like a sheaf of corn with all the ears fallen around him.'

Big Horn was the worst defeat ever inflicted on American troops by Native Americans. When the relief column arrived two days later, they found a scene of horror. The bodies of hundreds of men and horses lay in tangled heaps, the corpses of the humans stripped naked and mutilated.

In the midst of this carnage stood one survivor, Comanche.

The horse had stayed close to the body of Keogh, blood oozing from a dozen rifle and arrow wounds in his flanks and neck. The headband of his bridle had been cut loose, the bit lolled out of his mouth and his saddle had slipped under his belly. The Indians had taken dozens of surviving horses for their own use, but had ignored Comanche. Perhaps they thought he was as good as dead.

The first instinct of the relief force was to put an end to Comanche's misery. One swift shot and his pain would be over. However, the farrier, Gustave Horn, looked him over again and thought there was a ray of hope since none of his injuries had touched a vital organ. One bullet had even gone straight through his neck without doing serious damage. Still shattered by what they had found, the troopers resolved that come hell or high water Comanche would live.

When his wounds were dressed, the stricken horse was gently led 15 miles to the mouth of the Little Big Horn River. Troopers walked either side of him all the way, ready to catch him if he stumbled. At the river mouth the steamship *Far West* was waiting to evacuate casualties. Once on board Comanche was bedded down under a canvas awning on the after deck. Then followed a 51-hour trip downstream to Fort Bismarck. From there he was taken to Fort Lincoln, the home of the Seventh Cavalry.

The Battle of Little Big Horn had sent shockwaves across the USA. What the Native Americans thought of as a great victory, the white men called a massacre. For the United States, Comanche became a symbol of hope rising from tragedy and the nation keenly followed his progress. For a year the mustang rested in the veterinary hospital, his weight supported by slings. Slowly, careful nursing brought him back to health.

## *Regimental Mascot*

As soon as he could walk, Comanche was given the freedom to wander where he wished about the fort. And the troopers soon had him spoiled. He had two favourite haunts: the officers' quarters, where he was sure there was a good supply of sugar lumps, and the canteen, where he was guaranteed a bucket of beer. At times, if the cooks had been too generous, he was seen to stagger back to his stall. In spite of his comfortable retirement, Comanche remained a war-horse at heart. When the bugle sounded for the squadrons to assemble, Comanche would sometimes trot to his old place in 'I' Troop.

On 10 April 1878 Colonel Sturgis issued special orders:

1. The horse known as 'Comanche', being the only living representative of the bloody tragedy of the Little Big Horn . . . his kind treatment and comfort should be a matter of special pride on the part of the Seventh Cavalry.
2. The Commanding Officer of 'I' Troop will see that a comfortable stall is fitted up for Comanche. He will not be ridden again by any person whatever, under any circumstances, nor will he be put to any kind of work.
3. Hereafter, upon all occasions of ceremony Comanche, saddled, bridled and led by a mounted trooper of Troop 'I', will be paraded with the regiment.

After this the 25th June became an official day of mourning for the Seventh Cavalry and every year until his death Comanche led the ceremonies. He trotted out at the head of Keogh's old troop, draped in black, with the stirrups reversed.

In 1888 the Seventh moved to Fort Riley and of course Comanche went with them. But even old heroes have to die. His peaceful retirement came to an end on 6 November 1891 when he was 29. The vet commented that he died 'from colic and general debility'. His body was preserved and put on display in the Museum of Kansas University. Comanche was still so famous that the University put his remains on show at the Chicago World's Fair in 1893, where he became one of the most popular exhibits.

## *Native American Protests*

Think about the Comanche story from a Native American point of view. The old horse was hailed as the sole survivor of Little Big Horn. But of course he wasn't: the Native Americans had won and most of them survived . . . for a while at least. After the battle however, the Americans took a grim revenge – Native Americans living peacefully on reservations were treated as prisoners of war, while so-called 'wild Indians' were hunted down. In the years after 1876 thousands died, their lands were taken and Native American resistance was broken.

In 1971 Native American students at Kansas claimed the old horse was a 'racist symbol' of the cruelties done to their people by the white men. They demanded that he be sent back to the army. However, the Native Americans lost this second battle of Little Big Horn. After a heated argument, the University authorities refused to part with Comanche and he can still be seen proudly standing in his glass case in the museum.

# Railway Jack, the Trained Baboon

## Train Pains

Ever had that sinking feeling on a station platform? The loudspeaker crackles into life and a muffled voice booms out, 'The 10:15 train for blah, calling at blap, blip and blop is now running three days late. We apologize for the delay. You are welcome to pitch your tents on the wasteground behind the station.'

'Oh dear me,' you say out loud (because you are a very polite person and wouldn't dream of using rude words). 'Somebody has been monkeying about with the trains again.'

Now supposing you found out that a monkey, or rather a baboon, really was working for the railway company. And that the ape was in charge of . . . operating the signals! Would you be keen to get on a train again? Not likely. Well, that was the situation facing passengers of the Cape Government Railways in South Africa in the

1880s. At first they protested loudly, unnerved at the sight of this strange signalman. Letters were written declaring that 'the ape should be discharged at once . . .' and 'this state of affairs is outrageous'. But when the full story was told, Jack the baboon became a firm favourite with travellers.

## *Working on the Railway*

The human hero of this tale is James Edwin Wide. In the 1870s he left England to seek a better life in South Africa. He soon found a job as a labourer on the railway, laying the line from Uitenhage to Graaff-Reinet – but then his luck ran out. In 1877 James was knocked down by a train. If this was a novel James would have rolled out of the way and escaped, only it isn't, and real heroes are not always lucky. He had both legs cut off just below the knees.

James survived but he was crippled. For most workers in Victorian times this would have been a complete disaster. There were few jobs for disabled people. Unusually James's employers decided to give him a chance. He was kept on the payroll as a signalman at Uitenhage. If he could cope with the work . . .

Wide was not a quitter – he knew a job meant wages and independence. He had to manage somehow! The first problem, however, was travelling to work. His cottage was a long walk from the signal box, following a path by the side of the railway line. A very long walk on peg legs and crutches. At first he bravely paced it out, arriving sweating and exhausted each day. But he knew he couldn't keep it up. Already his stumps were chafed and bleeding. Something had to be done – or he'd have to resign before he was sacked.

The something was a flash of brilliance. James designed and built himself a four-wheeled trolley to run along the lines. Even better, he trained a large mongrel dog to tow it.

'This is marvellous,' he thought, 'I get to work much quicker and I'm not worn out. Now, if only I could think of a way of making the signalling easier? That distant signal is three-quarters of a mile away and can be really stiff . . . and then there is all the moving around and standing up . . .' (The levers at the signal box were attached to the signal by cables. The further away the signal, the harder the lever was to pull.)

## Helping Hands

One morning in 1881, James saw a sad-looking, young baboon for sale in the market. Baboons were common in South Africa and it was not unusual to see one on sale alongside ducks, geese and hens. Baboons were strong and intelligent, even though they could be ferocious. Some were even used in bloody fights with dogs – a cruel sport James hated.

He looked at the miserable ape and couldn't resist the appeal in its eyes. And then he had his second brainwave moment! With patience and kindness the animal could be the answer to his prayers. 'I think you might just do, young fellow,' he whispered soothingly to the baboon as he handed over the cash. It was the beginning of a great partnership.

Wide christened his new companion Jack. The baboon was bright, eager to please and affectionate. The two quickly became firm friends. Within a few months Jack was working hard for his disabled master and they settled into a routine that lasted for nine years.

Each day began early, pumping water, tidying the house and sharing breakfast. After that, man and ape prepared for the journey to work. Jack learned to lift the trolley onto the track, pushing and twisting it until the wheels were mounted securely on the rails. When James was comfortably seated, Jack locked the door to the cottage and handed him the key.

At first Jack helped the dog pull the trolley. He wore a leather belt around his waist, and a chain ran between this and a hook on one of Wide's wooden legs. The two excitedly towed their master to the signal box, the best of rivals. Sadly an accident brought an end to this unusual team – one morning the dog was killed by a passing train.

This left Jack with a monkey puzzle – how was he to move James on his own? After a little thought and experiment he made a discovery. If he gripped the tracks with his feet, and braced

his arms against the trolley, he could push his master along much quicker than he could pull him. Even better, Jack realized, when the trolley was on a downgrade he could jump aboard and skim along on a free ride.

The baboon learned as quickly at the signal box as he had at the cottage. Soon, when an engine driver blew his whistle, all James had to do was call out the name of the lever to be pulled. At the command 'Home' or 'Distant' Jack sprang up, operated the signal and pushed it back into place when the train had passed. James even taught him to carry out his own safety checks. Each time he used a lever, Jack looked along the line to make sure the signal arm had moved.

Another of James's duties was to look after the 'coal' key. This was the key to the padlock which 'locked off' the points that led to the coal yard. He kept it handy, hanging from a nail in the signal box. When an engine came down the main line for coal, the driver gave four blasts on his whistle. This was the signal that he wanted to open the points. As soon as James heard the whistle he took the key from the nail, came out of the box and hobbled to the edge of the platform. As the engine steamed slowly by he handed it over to the driver. On the return journey the driver gave four more blasts, cut his speed to a crawl, and returned the key.

For a time Jack had watched this complicated procedure with interest. His eyes followed his master's every move . . . pick up the key . . . leave the box . . . hand it over to the driver . . . wait for the engine to come back again. Easy. One day when four whistles sounded Jack jumped up before James could move, snatched the key and handed it over to the astonished driver. James watched open-mouthed as the baboon waited patiently for the train to return, collected the key and hung it up again. Jack's eyes lit up with delight. 'What's the problem?' he seemed to say as

he scampered over for a scratch – his favourite reward. From then on this job was his too.

## The Inspector Calls

As news of 'Railway Jack' spread, he became a celebrity, so much so that trains slowed down to look at the strange signalman. Some passengers were delighted to see him pulling the trackside levers, but others were alarmed.

A monkey on the railway? What was the company thinking of?

★

James's employers had known about his useful pet for some time and been prepared to turn a blind eye. After all, there had been no complaints from other staff about James Wide's work. However, they couldn't ignore public concerns. An inspector was sent out from Uitenhage to investigate. If he had any doubts Jack would have to go.

Have you ever had an inspection at school? The teachers making polite conversation with the inspectors. You know what James went through then. For several nerve-racking hours the official watched Jack at work and then went away to make his report. The wait for his verdict was excruciating, but it was a triumph for baboon power when it finally arrived.

*Dear Mr Wide,*
*The Company wish to inform you that . . . blah blah blah . . . Jack made assistant signalman . . . blah blah blah . . . asset to the railway . . . put on payroll forthwith . . . remittance of 9d (4p) per day . . . plus half bottle of beer on Saturdays . . . blah blah blah . . . Well Done.*

After this stamp of approval the objections stopped. Indeed reassured by the inspection, travellers on the line took Jack to their hearts and spotting him became a high point of any journey.

Jack was appointed an assistant signalman just in time. Shortly after the inspection James went to check out the points. He guessed they were jammed by a stone that needed clearing. As he crossed the line, he stumbled, crashed down and hurt his arm. Until he recovered, all the signal box duties fell on Jack, but the baboon carried them out without a single mistake.

## Don't Monkey with my Master

Neighbours often dropped in on James and Jack and were astounded at how close they became — at least as close as any man and dog. George Howe wrote: 'It was very touching to see Jack's fondness for his master. As I drew near they were sitting on the trolley, one of the baboon's arms around his master's neck, the other stroking his face . . . With a touch as light as a woman's he brushed a speck of dust off James's trousers, all the while keeping up an incessant chatter.'

Yet for all Jack's training and gentleness he could become as fierce as a wild ape if James or he were threatened. There are two reports of 'wild Jack'. On one occasion another railwayman quarrelled with James, and raised his arms and his voice to him. Jack saw these threatening gestures and attacked instantly. He pushed and jostled the man off the platform. Confronted with an angry, screeching and leaping baboon the man wisely backed away.

The second incident began as a good-natured romp. A burly railway foreman called by, dressed in his best Sunday clothes, including a sparkling white shirt. He admired Jack and began to play with him. In a rough game of push and shove he hustled the baboon to the edge of the platform. Jack was delighted and pushed excitedly back, so much so that the foreman toppled over and landed badly, winding himself.

With that, the man lost his temper and filled the air with ripe oaths. 'Damned monkey . . . strangle . . . pull tail out . . . hairy devil.' You know the kind of thing. Bent on revenge, he picked up a stout stick and charged at the baboon. 'Great,' thought Jack. 'This game gets better and better. If he can have a weapon, so can I.'

Rising to the challenge, he grabbed an old coal sack, battering his enemy valiantly with it. In a flurry of black, choking dust the foreman retreated, his Sunday clothes much the worse for wear. And oohh that shirt!

On 9 April 1890 Jack died after being ill with tuberculosis for six months. James was broken-hearted. Yet in a way Jack lived on. Long after his death neighbours still talked about him, so much so that the director of the museum in Port Elizabeth decided to find out all he could about this remarkable ape. In the 1920s he interviewed over 25 people who remembered Jack, and he even talked to James Wide himself, then an old man. Using those interviews he wrote the first version of the baboon's story and made 'Railway Jack' famous throughout the world.

## Recommended Reading

F. W. Fitzsimmons was the director of the museum in Port Elizabeth. He wrote an article called *Jack, the Signalman Baboon* in the Cape Mercury, 29 May 1923. Give these details to your local library and they will be able to order you a copy of the original page of the newspaper from the British Library. Not only do you get Jack's story, but details of a 700-mile cattle drive by South African cowboys.

# *Elephant Stampede*

## *The Chesterfield Sprint*

**H**ow fast can you run? Bet you could go faster if you were being chased by four elephants or – even worse – four frightened, out of control, trumpeting, want-to-stamp-on-something-now elephants. Elephants so wild that they could smash through walls, hurt themselves badly and not even know they were injured. That was the unlucky fix George Lockhart found himself in one morning, sometime around 1903.

At first everything had been fine. George had collected the elephants from their stables in Chesterfield and was walking them to the theatre. They were strolling peacefully down a narrow lane when a gang of local children saw the troop coming. Excited and playful they scampered over – and then one shouted, 'Boo!'

OK, think about it. Why do you shout 'Boo'? A way of saying 'Hello'? Nope.

A signal that you are going to share your chocolate with your friends? Nope.

A short, loud word to frighten people? Yes!

Well, be warned, 'Boo' works on elephants too. And look at it from the pachyderms' (elephants') point of view. That bright Edwardian morning they were going to work, minding their own business, when suddenly, some snotty-nosed kid yells in their sensitive ears. So what do they do? Something that elephants are very good at – panic.

As soon as the child yelled the fatal 'Boo', George knew he was in trouble. The lead elephant, Salt, was skittish. If she started to run the others would follow. To his dismay he watched her look about in shock and break into a lumbering charge. So what's the problem? Just get out of the way, George. Well, several really, you might like to rearrange them in order of priority.

The lane is narrow.
The elephants are big.
George is in front of them.
. . . and to make the situation perfect:
They have just snapped their safety chains.

George summed up the dilemma in a split

second and did the only sensible thing — ran for his life. But what next?

If he tripped, he would be squashed.
If he stopped and shouted, 'Whoa, hold up, elephants,' he would be squashed.
If he tried to climb a wall, before he could reach the top he would be squashed.

So how on earth had he got into this pickle in the first place? Why was he taking four elephants for a walk? . . . to the theatre? . . . in Chesterfield?

To find out the answers, let's leave George to his Olympic dash while we go back in time, to the last years of Queen Victoria's reign, God bless her.

## Circus Blood

George belonged to a circus clan. There had been Lockharts circusing about since circuses began — but his father, also called George, was to blame for the elephants. (To save confusion in the rest of the story, from now on we'll call our hero Little George and his dad Big George.)

When Little George was born in 1887, there were already three elephants at the family home in Brighton — Boney, Molly and Waddy. (Guess what the Lockharts called their house? Elephanta Lodge . . . Yes really.)

As a toddler he was brought up with these three big 'sisters' and soon learned the many dangers of being near them. One essential thing was drummed into him by his father: 'Listen to this vital rule, George. Never get between an elephant and a wall – or one elephant and another elephant. Elephants can bang against each other without doing themselves any harm but if a boy is in the way, the result might be instant, squished Little George.'

In spite of the risks of caring for them, these three were the good elephants (wait for it – the bad ones are coming soon). They were young, female Indian elephants who learned their tricks patiently and pleasantly. As Big George, the ring master, would have said, 'My lords, ladies, gentleman and children, we present for your delectation . . .'

### Trick 1 Follow My Leader
When given the command 'Tails', the elephants became a living chain, walking in line holding one another's tails with their trunks.

### Trick 2 The World's First Cycling Elephant
Boney, the smallest elephant, learned to ride a tricycle. It was made of steel, weighed over 50 kilos and had a tiller, like a boat, instead of

handlebars. Boney sat in the large saddle, peddled furiously and steered by holding the tiller with her trunk.

### Trick 3 Giant Skittles

These were just the highlights – other show-stoppers included see-sawing elephants, cannon-firing elephants and an elephant band. In the last years of the nineteenth century, Little George grew into a young man, touring the world with the family show. The performances took place in traditional big tops but also in theatres and music halls. In the days before cinema, animal acts were all the rage.

Audiences from Russia to the USA were stunned by the Lockharts' amiable, agile beasts and the family made a fortune. So much so, that in 1901, Big George decided it was time to retire. The elephants were sold for the princely sum of £2,000 and with tears in his eyes, Little George, now fourteen, watched Boney, Molly and Waddy walk away with their new owner, politely holding 'tails'. His childhood friends were gone.

## A Trunk Full of Troubles

The Lockharts were now rich, comfortable and within a few months – bored. Yawningly bored. Big George hated retirement so much that within a few months he decided he had made a terrible mistake. Desperate to return to circus life he bought a new troupe of four elephants – and a trunk full of troubles.

To look at, the new elephants seemed fine. Like the old troupe they were infant females and the Lockharts called them Salt, Pepper, Mustard and Sauce. They had recently been captured in the Far East and the marks of the catchers' ropes were still around their ankles. They should have been fresh and eager, without any bad habits picked up from poor trainers or ill treatment. And certainly, they learned their tricks quickly, soon standing on their hind legs for a juicy carrot.

So far so good, but a hidden problem lurked in the wings and almost turned their first show into a disaster. The elephants were easily scared. Shortly after their performance began, the new troupe turned tail and bolted from the circus ring. Little George was standing close by but he had no idea what had startled them. He hadn't seen or heard anything strange but luckily he reacted quickly. He recalled years later, 'Trying to stop them I grabbed the ears of the leading pair and hung on. They crashed along with my body hanging between their heads. Nothing stopped them, not even stout doors. I was very glad that their foreheads were in advance of my body or they would have squashed me on the first door.'

He clung on with a vice-like grip until they ran out of steam, then led them back in triumph.

Unfortunately for both George Lockharts this breakout was only the first. Salt, Pepper, Mustard and Sauce could be as sour as their names suggested. As Little George put it, 'They were like April weather, either sunshine or rain, and we never knew which to expect.'

At worst the elephants were a danger to themselves – and everyone around them.

## Like a Bomb in a Sweet Shop

The second serious stampede happened in a London theatre. As Lockharts' elephants waited calmly for their turn to go on stage both Georges were relaxed. A troupe of Russian dancers was performing. This was an act they hadn't seen before and father and son watched them with a professional eye.

Have you seen Russian dancers on TV? Balaikas playing, Cossacks leaping about – familiar??

Can you remember how they often end an energetic dance??? Yes – with a deafening yell. 'Oi Vladivostok – Shostakovich' or something very Russian. What was the effect on the nice calm elephants? Panic. Stampede.

Salt took off and the others careered after her, pell-mell. Even the biggest theatres were not renowned for the amount of space backstage and performers scattered out of the way. Except for one young woman. She watched the elephants bearing down on her and froze. Little George, with an almost superhuman effort, hurled himself forward, grabbed her by the waist and threw her out of the way.

[Romantic Pause: Their eyes lingered in their endangered embrace and – bet you can guess the next corny bit. You've got it, they fall in love and marry. What a story for the best man to tell at the wedding. 'Now let me remind you how the happy couple were introduced – by a small herd of charging elephants.' Right, slushy part over, back to the story.]

Outside the theatre the elephants split up and barged their way through the busy crowds. Mustard, lost and confused, charged into a sweet shop with George in panting pursuit. Inside, she found herself trapped by the sturdy wooden counter and tried to push past into the parlour behind. Frantically, she waved her trunk and sent neat rows of jars flying. As humbugs hummed through the air, the brave shopkeeper slammed the counter down and yelled 'Shoo' at the large invader.

When Little George stepped in he was horrified. Mustard was caught fast, but if she panicked again she would tear the place apart.

Hoping that his voice had a confident tone that he did not feel, he spoke soothingly to her. Luckily, after a few last glass-shattering twitches of her trunk, she stood still. Now, how to get her out of this tight spot?

'Back,' Little George ordered.

Nothing.

'Back, girl.'

No response.

'Back, Mustard.'

Zilch elephant movement.

'Back . . . Back . . . Back . . . Back!' he yelled until he was hoarse. Whether she was stuck or stubborn, Mustard was going nowhere.

Suddenly Little George had an idea.

'The floor isn't big enough for her to move,' he told the grim shopkeeper. 'But if I can get her feet up on your counter she will probably turn round.'

He was either brave, or just desperate, but when Little George reached for one great grey foot, the shopkeeper bent down to lift the other. Guided by the men, Mustard stood her front feet on the counter and edged her body forward. Encouraged, Little George jumped up beside her and heaved her head towards the door. Squealing and protesting, she edged round, scattering more tins, jars and boxes. As he eased Mustard out of the shop, Little George glanced back and blushed. It looked as if a bomb had exploded inside.

Taking the elephant by the ear, George led her back to the stables and then went to help his dad. He found Big George and the other three runaways in a cemetery. Big George was sitting on a tombstone, his face running with sweat, but far from downhearted.

'Come on, George,' he snapped, looking at his watch. 'There's still time for a performance.' And in the best show business tradition, Lockhart's Elephants went on as the finale to deafening applause.

## Don't be Cruel to the Elephants, George

After the theatre break-out the Georges had words – quite heated ones. Little George was convinced that one day there would be a disaster with the elephants if they didn't work out a way of stopping them when they stampeded. And he knew how to do it – a safety rope.

He had tried leading Salt, with a rope tied to one of her forelegs. It was a bit like taking an overgrown dog for a walk. Of course, if she started to run he couldn't hold her back but he had discovered a simple way of bringing her to a grinding halt. If he dropped the rope Salt stepped on it, tripped herself, and fell onto her knees. Ingenious, what? But his father wouldn't hear of it.

'That would be cruel to the animal, George,' he declared. 'And cruelty to my elephants I will not tolerate. I think we shall be all right in the future.'

## Back to the Chesterfield Stampede

It's a good job Big George stuck to circuses and hadn't tried to make his living as a fairground fortune teller. He wasn't good at predicting what would happen next. Shortly after their disagreement Little George was not 'all right', he was racing for his life down an alley in Chesterfield – with no rescuing rope to drop.

With his lungs bursting George dashed on until he realized (gasp) that (gasp) the elephants (gasp) were no longer behind him (gasp . . . gasp). Looking back he saw them swerve through a gate into a hotel yard. Saved? Yes! Emergency over? Er . . . no, about to get worse actually. As Little George whirled round and flung himself into the yard, he saw Salt and her gang smash through a gate on the opposite side. Behind them was a scene of mayhem.

A pony harnessed to a trap (a small carriage)

was rearing and shrieking. The passengers, two old ladies, sat slumped in their seats, since both had swooned in terror. As the trap swung and bucked it seemed certain they would be thrown to the ground. George cursed — he knew he had to stop and help them, but the elephants would be miles away by the time he had finished. As he hesitated, he saw a stableman rush from the hotel to steady the pony. Thankful that the old ladies were safe, George shot through the shattered door after his own wayward animals.

The sight that awaited him was not good. Salt was leading the others on a rampage through a row of back gardens. The gardens were separated by 2-metre walls but these meant little to the elephants. They broke through each one in turn, like swimmers cresting waves of brick. In the distance however, Little George thought he spied hope. At the end of the row was a substantial building, maybe a factory. 'Ah,' he yelled at the grey backs leaping ahead of him, 'now that will stop you.'

Yet as he closed in, the elephants thought otherwise. They charged this new barrier together. As Little George watched, the wall began to bulge, masonry and bricks loosening and dropping. With a crash it collapsed and they were through. Trumpeting wildly they surged inside, and disappeared. Carefully, Little George peered in over a pile of rumble. Were they trapped at last? The answer came with another juddering crunch, as the tearaways burst out the other side.

Scrambling through, Little George found himself in a rope-walk – a long thin factory for spinning ropes. Stunned workers stood open-mouthed, gawping at the escape hatch the elephants had just made for themselves. And can you blame them? That morning, ho-hum, work was going on as normal, ho-hum. A rope for a ship; a rope for a mine, hum-drum. When smash – enter charging elephants, crash – exit charging elephants. Was this real?

Dashing through the rope-walk before the workmen could recover, Little George found himself in a field, with a boundary wall ahead. The elephants were already halfway across, but this time he had no illusions that a simple wall would stop them. Sure enough they tore it apart, yet for once pachyderm power was in for a shock. To his relief, their charge was rudely broken. On the other side of the wall, the ground dropped sharply, only a metre or so, but this was all that was needed. Down they sprawled, turning incredible somersaults. Picture it, four times four tons of spinning elephants.

As Little George caught up once more, the dazed beasts scrambled to their feet and decided to

head for cover. Again sneaky Salt, the leader of the escape committee, led the way. Their target was a large wooden hut. Little George glanced round for help and thankfully saw his father running up, but he wasn't bringing good news. Big George was yelling urgently, 'Stop them. Stop them going into that hut. It's full of old machinery. They'll cut themselves to tatters!'

'Thanks, Dad,' he mumbled to himself. 'What do you think I've been trying to do for the last twenty minutes?' But he knew he couldn't stand still and watch the elephants injure themselves, even if they deserved it. Without any clear plan in mind he sped towards the shed, cutting in front of the animals. With a lung-wrenching burst of speed, Little George barely managed to beat the herd to the door of the shed and . . . well what could he do? He trusted to the elephants' common sense. Surely they would recognize him if he was in front of them – facing them. Surely if he yelled at them and waved his arms furiously they would stop or turn aside? Surely?? Surely???

Argh! Help! . . . Help! The elephants were now so spooked that any ele-sense had long since gone. Salt head-butted Little George and he fell back into the hut, winded. Terrified, he stared up at what must surely be his last sight on earth – Salt coming through the door to trample him. As he waited for the crushing feet to pound the life out of him, she reared and . . . stopped.

Was this a miracle? Well, yes of a kind. As Salt started to enter the hut, a second elephant decided to join in the fun. The two pressed forward together and they jammed. Jammed tight against each other in the door frame. Trumpeting in frustration, they shook and struggled until it seemed the hut would fly apart, but the stout timbers held. And as suddenly as the mad stampede had started, it finished. Big George arrived and gave stern-voiced commands, just as the elephants began to tire. Confused and a little afraid, they calmed down and meekly held tails, ready to be led away.

In the following days the invoices for damage flowed in to the Lockharts' hotel, and they were many and big. 'Dear Sir, I wish to complain at the outrageous damage done to my wall, gate, factory, garden, lawn, granny . . . The repair will cost £2, £3, £5, £15, £20, £30 . . .' Big George went white.

Was this the end of Lockhart's circus? Brought to its knees by an outraged public. Surprisingly not! There is nothing like a whiff of danger to excite an audience. For every person that complained in Chesterfield there were 100 who had heard about the rampage, and wanted to see the runaway giants. Shows were packed and the box-office takings huge – far more than the cost of paying the bills.

The Lockharts and their new elephants went on to be stars of Edwardian England once again. But they always kept one eye open for the next time Salt and her moody gang would plunge themselves into danger. 'It's time,' thought Little George to himself, 'for another chat with Dad about that safety rope.'

## Big George's best memory – A Royal Performance

Big George had a favourite story. In the days of Boney, Molly and Wally, Lockhart's Elephants performed for five summer seasons at the Crystal Palace in London. This was the wonderful iron and glass structure built for the Great Exhibition in 1851, a great favourite of Londoners until it was burnt down in 1936.

One afternoon the Prince and Princess of Wales came to see the show and thoroughly enjoyed themselves. As they were leaving, the Prince caught a glimpse of Little George's mother, dressed in her circus clothes. She was wearing tights, top boots, an embroidered tunic and a hat with a long feather.

'Come here, little boy,' he called to her. 'You seem very young to work with such large elephants.' Then His Royal Highness, who always had an eye for a pretty girl, noticed his error. As she curtseyed, he laughed and complimented her. 'Well, well. You are the smartest boy-girl I've ever seen.' As the Lockharts were to find, the visit lingered in the Prince's memory because of the amusing mistake he had made.

Years later, Big George was walking the troupe

through the busy city streets to perform at the London Pavilion. As they reached Shaftesbury Avenue the police had stopped all the traffic — the royal coach was coming. As it drew close the carriage came to an abrupt halt and the Prince, now King Edward VII, leaned out of the window to summon a policeman.

'Let Lockhart through,' he ordered. 'We must not keep the elephants waiting.'

Big George proudly led the elephants in front of the King's coach, raising his hat respectfully as he passed. In the circus world there was nothing to beat a satisfied audience.

# Whale Wars

**W**hales are the largest mammals on earth and statistics about them are mind-boggling. Ready to be boggled?

## Walloping Big Facts About Whales

- The blue whale, the largest species, grows to over 30 metres in length and weighs as much as 2,000 men.
- A baby blue whale will drink more than 425 litres of milk a day.
- The brain of the sperm whale, at 9 kilos, is six and a half times the size of a human brain.
- The song of the humpback whale can be heard over 1,000 miles of open ocean.
- The killer whale can reach speeds of 60 kilometres an hour, the fastest creature in the sea.
- Grey whales migrate over 7,000 miles from the Arctic waters of Alaska to the coast of Mexico — the longest migration of any mammal on earth.
- The bowhead whale has a mouth the size of a cathedral door — big enough for two elephants to enter side by side.

You have got to admit whales are impressive. So how have people treated these amazing creatures? Slaughtered them for hundreds of years, of course.

For most of history the war between humans and whales was dangerous for both sides. Whales were tracked and killed by men in small wooden boats, armed with hand-thrown harpoons. However, technology turned hunting into massacre. In the twentieth century, whales stood no chance against powerful, steel-hulled ships and explosive harpoons, fired from cannons.

By the 1960s, whales had been hunted so heavily and so ruthlessly that most species were in danger of being wiped out. With a jolt, public opinion woke up to the problem and governments began to take notice. In 1972 the United Nations Conference on the Human Environment voted 52-0 in favour of banning all commercial whaling. Over the next ten years a quota was set for the number of whales each nation could kill each year. Finally, in 1986 whaling was banned. A ban that has continued, but only just.

This is a story linking two whales. They lived in different times and different oceans, but they had one thing in common – they fought back against their human hunters. Be warned! If you like happy endings skip this chapter. If you love brave animals read on . . .

## Moby Dick, the Demon Whale

The most famous whale story in the world, *Moby Dick*, was written by the American author Herman Melville in 1850. In his novel, the crew of the whaling ship *Pequod* hunt the ferocious Moby, a monstrous white whale. The unlucky sailors are led to a watery doom by Ahab, their mad captain.

Melville strikes fear into his readers by recounting Moby's awesome and almost supernatural powers. His ghostly white head and hump give warning that he has come to do battle; he is huge, with a distinctive twisted lower jaw; harpoons seem unable to hurt him, but worst of all is his evil intelligence. He pretends to flee, lures boats within striking distance and then turns to smash them. Yet Melville's creepy book is based on fact. He was inspired by the true story of Mocha Dick.

## Mocha Dick, the White Whale of the Pacific

Let's begin, like salty old sea dogs, with our charts. The island of Mocha lies off the coast of Chile in latitude 38 28' south. The seas around this beautiful island were the territory of Mocha Dick, the white avenger of whalekind. (Right, research. Atlas out, find Mocha. What do you mean you are not at school? Ever heard of a love of learning?)

In the early 1800s, Dick was an old bull sperm whale, of immense size and strength. He had survived a hundred fights with whalers and bore the scars. As his fame spread Dick became a target for every harpooner eager to make his reputation. When whale ships passed in the vast Pacific, they greeted one another with the message: Any news of Mocha Dick? And almost every captain who brought his vessel round Cape Horn, at least those who had the courage, swept down the coast of Chile to pit their skill against him.

As Mocha Island drew near, nervous look-outs clung to the mast-head and scanned the waves for signs of the 'monster'. At first glance he might be mistaken for a low cloud hugging the sea. But a wary eye knew better. Dick was a freak of nature, a huge sperm whale, as white as wool, his great head rugged with clustered barnacles.

As he glided through the water his spouts erupted in the air, as if his breathing was deeper than others of his kind. These roaring fountains marked his awesome progress — a sonorous monarch of the deep. The noise reminded dumbstruck sailors of the ear-splitting sound of steam escaping from the safety valve of an engine.

Yet Mocha Dick was not a danger unless he was provoked. Although he had been hunted many times, he held no grudges against men. He was often seen swimming lazily past whale boats with long and easy sweeps of his flukes (tail fins) — even as the harpooners took aim. It was only after the first blow was struck that Dick became a holy terror.

He turned on his tormentors with open jaws or flashing tail, crushing or smashing their tiny vessels. Men drowned or were battered to death by his fury. In one fight he cut off three English boats, destroying two as they turned and rowed for cover. The third was ground to pieces against the side of the mother ship, as the desperate crew tried to hoist it out of the water.

## The Nantucket Whaler

Dick's last battle was reported in 1839. Strangely, the name of the man who hunted him down wasn't given. He was simply called the Mate. But whatever you think about his bloody trade, his courage can't be doubted. He was the First Mate of an American ship, out from Nantucket — and Nantucket whalers reckoned they were the best.

The Mate was 35. His furrowed face made him look older, but the wrinkles marked 20 years of experience gained from the Tropics to the Polar Seas. He wasn't tall but what he lacked in height he made up in strength. His back was straight and his shoulders broad and hard. His arms were long and bulged with muscle — the mark of the job that thrilled him most. When it was time to hunt, he was a harpooner.

## Round One — A Draw

The Yankee whale ship had rounded Cape Horn and was running before a gentle breeze from the south. It was a perfect evening, the western sky flooded with amber light, the surface of the sea like waving gold. The Captain, prowling his quarter deck, saw it first — a lone spout. He scowled and cussed the dozing lookout, 'You leaden-eyed lubber! Lazy son of a sea cook! Come down, sir.'

'There she blows! Sperm whale. Lone bull, sir,' the lookout yelled, shame-faced, as he dropped from the crow's nest.

In a flurry of activity the crew made ready for the chase. Harpoons, ropes and water-kegs were thrown into the boats as the ship closed in. It was the boats that carried the harpooners to their grisly work. Before the harpoon was thrown, one end of a rope was tied to the haft. When the weapon was embedded in the whale, the other end was secured to the loggerhead of the boat, a stout timber post. This meant the dying whale had to tow its killers until its strength failed and it could be finished off.

'Back the main-top-s'l. There she blows,' yelled the Captain. 'Ready to lower all hands, every damned one of ye . . . Lower away.'

In an instant two boats were let down and the men scrambled into them. With a chorus of shouts and whoops the race began.

The First Mate, in charge of one tiny skiff, yelled encouragement. He was in no mood to come last.

'There she blows. Eighty barrels of the finest oil, boys, waiting to be towed alongside. Long and quick strokes. Now she feels the touch!'

And each mother's son pulled as if he had been born with an oar in his hand. They stretched every sinew for the glory of hurling the first harpoon.

As they neared the whale, the Mate's boat drew steadily ahead, but the target was elusive. At

15 metres only about a couple of centimetres of hump was above water – and then the bull dived. A pair of flukes six metres wide waved a brief farewell. Bobbing in the wake, the men lay on their oars to catch breath.

Time oozed slowly by and then a spout rose on the starboard side, a few hundred metres away. Before the Mate had time to react and order the boat turned, the bull attacked. Lashing the sea into a ferment with his tail, he bore down at full speed, 'jaws on'. As he surged forward, the men saw to their horror that the whale was as white as the surf he was churning. They were head to head with Mocha Dick.

'Mocha Dick or the devil, this crew never sheers off from anything that wears the shape of a whale. Pull easy, just enough to steer,' the Mate commanded.

His sharp words cut through their fear and the boat turned smoothly to meet the great beast.

This time, however, the Mate had made a mistake – he was steersman not harpooner. The young sailor with the harpoon was brave but daunted. He had heard the stories of Mocha Dick told on rum-soaked nights, and now, as the real leviathan tore towards him, his knees shook and his arm trembled. He threw strongly, but his aim was off-mark. His first shot barely grazed

Mocha Dick's back and the second missed altogether.

Briefly the whale kept up his charge, then, as if mocking the men for their childish efforts to hurt him, he dived again, only a few metres from their boat. The Mate was left seething and soaked in a storm of spray. Burning with anger he blasted the harpooner, 'Clumsy lubber. You a whalesman? You are fit only to spear eels. Cowardly spawn.'

The lad was so ashamed that he threw himself over the side and had to be dragged fighting and kicking back on board. As he dripped miserably, night closed in and the disgruntled whalers rowed slowly back to their ship.

## *Round Two – A Blow Struck*

'There they breech. About a league off (4 kilometres); heads same as we do.'

The Captain went aloft to see for himself and smiled as he gave orders: 'Sperm whale and a thundering big school of them. Get in the craft; swing the cranes.' Good, no sign of Mocha Dick, he thought, and plenty of easy meat.

In a twinkling the boats, three this time, were launched and the hunt was on. As they neared, the school dived but in the sharp light of a fine day the Mate could see their path under water.

'Follow me,' he called to the other boats, 'they swim fast but we'll be among them when they rise.'

After a mile of hard rowing they stopped and waited, but nothing broke the surface. Five minutes passed, then they saw it – a lone calf playing in the sunshine. Perfect! Its distress calls would echo through the ocean.

'Pull up and strike it,' the Mate commanded the boat nearest to the youngster. 'It may bring up the old one – perhaps the whole school.'

The plan worked. The harpoon bit deep and when the calf made its first agonized plunge, the cow surfaced. She tried desperately to protect her pup, and took it under her fin. But it was too late. Although she tried to coax the calf to safety, it rolled over and died. The tenderness of the mother meant nothing to the whalers, except the chance of a second kill. As she thrashed the sea in sorrow, the harpooner struck again. The cow had become a victim herself, her blood staining the sea.

Yet the Mate had no time to watch the outcome of this one-sided struggle. A mile distant another whale had 'breached'. As the spray settled the Mate muttered, 'I know you, my friend.' Mocha Dick was back and lashing towards the boat that had killed the calf. Was it coincidence or had he come to protect his species? The men had no doubt. 'He's making for the bloody water,' they cried.

Not a few hearts sank as they watched the white whale bear down on their shipmates. His flukes churned the sea and left a wake a rod wide (5m). Surely this was the time to row for their lives, but retreat was not a word the Mate understood. 'Harpooner,' he yelled, 'give me the dart and you steer. May the "Goneys" eat me if he dodges us this time. Pull for the red water.

We'll fight him in the blood of his own kind.'

No sooner had the Mate spoken than Mocha Dick came to a halt and seemed to lose interest in the men. The Mate did not return the favour. 'The old sog's (bull) lying to. Spring, boys and we have him. All my clothes and tobacco shall be yours, only lay me alongside that whale.'

As his boat closed, he aimed and threw. The harpoon hit hard and deep – and now the death struggle had begun. If Mocha Dick could lose his attackers he might survive the first wound. If the men could stay roped to the harpoon they could wear Dick down and spear him again.

## Round Three – Death of a Champion

As Dick felt the pain of the harpoon he exploded into action. Smashing down with fin and fluke he reared his barnacled head. The boat had barely a chance to row back a few strokes and miss the pounding blows. Then the white whale was off like a startled horse, surging between shallow dives and short skims above the waves. The line smoked as it ran through the chocks, in danger of being ripped away, until it was tied fast to the loggerhead. Now wherever Mocha Dick went, the men would go too.

For long minutes Dick ripped across the sea,

as if his strength was boundless. Yet the spray
behind him was stained red, the sign of a deep
wound. Finally he paused, his huge body
quivering, and the men took their chance.
Hauling on the rope, they pulled the boat close
and the Mate struck again with a second
harpoon, just under the shoulder.

At first Dick seemed to shrug the blow off . . . not even to feel it. He lay still on the water in an eerie silence, as if dozing. Then the pain hit – and with the shock another maddened rush. Leaping towards the boat, he crash-dived only a few metres short of the stern. The wash swept over the crew and, as they wiped the spray from their eyes, they saw that the steersman was missing. Dick had caught the long steering oar and flicked the unfortunate oarsman into the sea. Worse, as the whale continued to dive he was sucked down like a feather in a whirlpool.

Anxiously, the others scanned the surface for signs of life, beginning to doubt they would ever see him again. Had he taken a deep breath? How much air could a man hold in his lungs? Surely no one could last this long? Just as hope was fading, his head broke the surface and he was hauled aboard, panting and exhausted.

But that was only the first problem solved. Dick was still diving – and the boat was still tied to the harpoon. Two hundred fathoms (350 metres) of line had been carried spinning through the chocks, so fast that steam was rising from the damp fibres. Worse, the rope was about to run out and drag them under.

'Cut', hissed the Mate. 'Cut the line or he'll take us down.'

The nearest crewman drew his knife and tried

to hack them loose. It was no use. The rope was moving so quickly the knife flew out of his hand. And then the line had run its length. The stern jerked in the air as the bows were dragged under.

With cries and curses the crew made ready to jump, when abruptly the line slackened. With a thump the boat fell back on her keel, half swamped. Exhausted, Mocha Dick had reached the limits of his dive and turned to rise. And upward he came, so fast that when he surfaced five metres of his body burst above the ocean.

Stunned by their luck, the men had hardly began to bail, and the steersman to mumble a prayer of thanks, when the battle began again. Dick swam furiously for half a kilometre, with such renewed energy, that the men challenged the Mate. Shouldn't they cut the line now? While they still could?

'Give me one more blow, me fine boys,' he pleaded. 'One more blow.'

The chance came quicker than he could have imagined. Mocha Dick stopped again, for no reason the crew could see. But the Mate could read the signs. Dick had halted, but his body was convulsing, as if hit by massive electric shocks.

'Haul on, me boys,' he ordered. As the boat touched he picked up the boat spade and drove it home – twice. The boat spade was an even crueller weapon than the harpoon. Shaped like a broad axe, it was used to cut pieces from living whales.

Now mortally wounded, Dick wheeled round to ram the boat, but fell short.

'Stern all,' yelled the Mate. 'Stern all before we are crushed.' As they backed away Dick began his death throes, beating the water with head and fluke. The Mate watched grimly as a stream of black, clotted blood showered from Mocha Dick's spout.

'There, thick as tar! Stern, boys! Stern every soul of ye! He's going in a flurry!'

For a minute longer Mocha Dick thrashed the sea that he had ruled, the sound of his blows like the fire of artillery. Then he rolled over, fin up – beaten at last.

Did Mocha Dick deserve his reputation as a monster of the deep? The Mate certainly believed so. Dick was the longest whale he had ever killed, more than 23 metres from his 'noddle to his flukes'. And had Dick really been at war with whalers for more than 30 years? The Nantucket men counted twenty rusting harpoons embedded in his flesh – above all else Dick had been a fighter.

# The Pirate Whaler

A hundred and forty years later, whales were protected by international law. But one problem with laws is that they have to be enforced. In the 1970s many whalers believed governments had no right to interfere with their work. After all, hadn't their fathers and grandfathers been whalers? And there was still plenty of money to be made while nations like the Japanese would buy all the whale meat they could get hold of – whether legal or illegal meat. From a host of countries – South Africa, Spain, Portugal, Chile, Peru, Korea and Taiwan – pirate whaling ships set sail. In July 1978 however, one greedy pirate vessel ran into more trouble than it could handle.

The *MV Tona* was a 540-ton converted trawler, operating out of the Canary Islands. Her papers said that she worked for the Red Mullet Fishing Company, a dummy company, set up to fool any investigations into the real work of the *Tona*. Under command of her tough Norwegian Skipper, Kristof Vesprehein, she cut a bloody swathe through the Atlantic Ocean. Any species, no matter how endangered, was caught and slaughtered. The prime meat was cut from the body and the carcass dumped back in the sea.

On 27 June the *Tona* set out on what proved

to be a successful hunt. Almost a month later, on July 22, she was returning to the Canaries with her freezers full of meat. At 5 pm, about 300 kilometres off the coast of Portugal, an enormous fin whale was sighted. Although his ship was low in the water with the weight of her cargo, Captain Vesprehein couldn't let such a prize go.

Fin whales swim fast and were almost impossible to catch in the ships of Mocha Dick's day. Vesprehein, however, faced no problems with wind and sails. Clutching the throttle, he revved his powerful diesel engines and soon overtook the whale. As soon as they were in range the harpooner took aim — and fired. Unlike the First Mate of old, his strength and bravery were not tested. The harpoon cannon blasted the deadly blade deep into the helpless animal. A steel cable was fastened to the harpoon and using an electric winch the crew began to haul the dying animal aboard.

So far all very hi-tech and one-sided — then the tables turned. The fin whale fought on, even as its life ebbed away. Winching the dying giant aboard was taking time and the sea was getting rougher. As it thrashed and writhed the *Tona* began to pitch from side to side. Remember, she was already low in the water!

Suddenly the ship rolled wildly in the swell

and the side rails were pushed under the waves. In the tropical heat the crew had neglected to close several hatches and portholes and the water cascaded down into the engine room.

This was a disaster! The engines cut out – and with them all the electrical power. The winch stopped and the *Tona* was trapped in a deadly clasp with the whale. The pirates could not release their catch, or cut it loose. The great body of the fin whale had become an anchor dragging the whaler ship to her doom.

As the seas poured in, the crew began to abandon ship, except for one. For whatever crazy reason Kristof Vesprehein stayed on the bridge – as if he couldn't really believe what was happening. With a bottle of beer in hand, he waved his men away, while he fought on to control the *Tona*. He died, ship's wheel in hand as she slipped into a watery grave. It was a rare victory for the whales.

## Whale Tales

### Alive in the belly of a whale! Read on if you have the stomach . . .

Ever wondered what it would be like to be swallowed by a whale? In 1891, English sailor James Bartley was swallowed by an angry whale during a hunt near the Falkland Islands in the

South Atlantic. Amazingly, he survived and described it like this:

'I remember very well the moment that I fell from the boat and felt my feet strike some soft substance. I looked up and saw a big ribbed canopy of light pink and white descended over me, and the next moment I felt myself drawn downward, feet first, and I realized that I was being swallowed. I was drawn lower and lower; a wall of flesh surrounded me and hemmed me on every side, yet the pressure was not painful and the flesh easily gave way, like soft india–rubber.

Suddenly I found myself in a sack much larger than my body, but completely dark. I felt about me; and my hands came in contact with several fishes, some of which seemed to be alive, for they squirmed in my fingers and slipped back to my feet. Soon I felt a great pain in my head and my breathing became more and more difficult. At the same time I felt a terrible heat . . . My eyes became coals in my head and I believed every moment I would perish . . . I tried to rise, to move my arms and legs, to cry out . . . I finally lost consciousness.'

How did James get out? The whale was killed and taken back to the ship. Several hours later, when the stomach was cut open James was found alive, but bleached a ghastly white by gastric acids.

### Good News for Whales

The hunting of whales has almost stopped and humans are doing more to protect them than ever before:

### Job Cuts Save the Whales

In 1998 a school that trained whales for the Russian navy was closed. The centre at Vityaz Bay, in the Far East, trained whales to detect divers and carry out suicide attacks against enemy shipping. The last five students – Bion, Mezon, Momon, Jerry and Bob – were transferred to a mammal research station in the Baltic Sea.

### Having a Whale of a Time

In the new millennium the world-wide whale business is booming. But these days it's based on whale-watching rather than hunting. The Mexicans were among the first to realize that more money could be made out of live whales than dead ones. In 1972 they set up the first whale sanctuary in the coastal lagoons of Baja, on the Pacific coast. These are the mating and calving grounds where the Californian grey whales end their 7,000-mile migration.

Now whale-watching has hit the web. An exciting site for the virtual whale watcher comes from Boston-based Wheelock and Simmons Colleges, which offer 'WhaleNet' at *http://www.wheelock.edu* to see pictures, on-line movies, hear whale song and read about whales of all sizes and species.

### 'Wall of Death' Nets Banned

European countries have agreed to ban the use of driftnets in the Mediterranean and Atlantic by 2002. Driftnets are 2.5 kilometres long and used to catch tuna and swordfish. However, they also trap any other large species in their path and have been nicknamed 'walls of death' by protesters. The environmental group Greenpeace estimates that thousands of sharks and dolphins are killed each year as unwanted 'by-catches' of the merciless nets. The fight goes on to ban them across the world.

# *The Tamworth Two*

*T*he British are a nation of pig lovers, or rather pork lovers. On average they eat 21 kg of pork and bacon, over a quarter of a big pig, every year. But what happens when the porkers become personalities? Be warned, if you enjoy a hot bacon sandwich reading this story may change your eating habits . . . for ever. This is the tale of three little pigs that tried to run all the way home.

## The Tamworth Two Escape the Chop

**Thursday 8 January, 1998**

Arnaldo Dijulio, a council road sweeper, was delivering two boars and a sow to Newman's Slaughterhouse in the small market town of Malmesbury, Wiltshire. He had bred and raised the pigs himself but he wasn't sentimental – he was looking forward to a full freezer. The animals had never been pets and he had always known what their fate would be – pork, ham and bacon joints. That day they were heading for apple sauce heaven.

Arnaldo had chosen the breed of his pigs carefully. He was not interested in common 'large whites' or broad 'saddlebacks' – he had selected old-fashioned Tamworths. Tamworths are one of the oldest breeds of British pigs – in fact an aristocrat of pigs. Although smaller than most other breeds, they taste delicious and Arnaldo knew that each of his five–month–old Tamworths weighed a mouth–watering 50 kg. The meat his family couldn't eat would be sold for a tidy profit.

But Arnaldo had forgotten other qualities of Tamworths. They are hardy and resourceful. With their long legs and bodies they can run fast and their ginger colouring makes excellent camouflage in wooded country. The blood of wild boars still flows in their veins and they are not afraid to give a human a nasty bite. The British Prime Minister, Winston Churchill, probably had Tamworths in mind when he said, 'Dogs look up at us. Cats look down at us. Pigs treat us as equals.'

When Arnaldo drove into Newman's yard he reversed the trailer holding the pigs up to the slaughterhouse door – but not quite close enough. The pigs smelt blood in the air and they knew in an instant they were for the chop. As the gate of the trailer was lowered, the Tamworths made a break for freedom.

Believe it or not, catching a charging pig isn't easy. In theory if you grab one by its ears you can drag it along — but would you like to get a grip on 50 kg of desperate porker? And what would you say when it looked you in the eye?

'Now look here, pig. Are you going to come quietly or do I have to get nasty?'
or perhaps something a little friendlier:

'Here, piggy, piggy, piggy. What nice teeth you have.'

Not sure you're up to it? And neither were the staff at Newman's. They rushed to shut the gates; they yelled a lot; they ran after the pigs waving their arms, but no one was going to try a rugby tackle on a Tamworth.

Two of the pigs, one boar and the sow, circled the yard grunting and squealing. They knew this was their only chance of escape and hastily scanned the ground. Then they saw it — a hole in the bottom of the fence. It wasn't quite large enough but that was no problem. Did you know that pigs can dig and that Tamworths are the miners of the pig world? Neither did Arnaldo. In a blur of trotters they were under the fence and away.

Peter Newman watched them go, but he was not especially worried. He knew his job. The company was a family firm, founded by his grandfather 50 years ago. Animals had escaped before and, at worst, this meant an annoying chase down the road before they were cornered. He smiled as he remembered a pig incident years ago. A cheeky boar had snatched a £5 note from its owner's hand and eaten it. When the animal was delivered to Newman's it came with a message that read: *Your fee is in the pig*.

Arnaldo and the men from the slaughterhouse

chased after the Tamworths, expecting to round them up quickly. But once again, they underestimated piggy cunning. Unlike a silly sheep or a complacent cow they didn't run down the road, they headed for open country. The wily pair scampered across a field and plunged into the River Avon. Arnaldo stood bewildered as his porkers surged across the river like Olympic swimmers and vanished into the fields on the other side.

Wait a moment! This was the story of three big piggies. Two are safe . . . so far . . . but what about number three? Sadly the third Tamworth never made it out of the slaughterhouse yard. He was cut off from the escape hole and captured. Nothing could save his bacon and as Newman's put it, he was 'processed in the usual way'. Now wipe that tear away and turn back to this crackling good story.

## The Tamworth Two go to Ground

Like the best commandos, the pigs lay low for a couple of days and lived off the countryside. Then sightings of the two tearaways began. Harry Clarke saw them rooting around his vegetable patch but he wasn't concerned. 'They were quite friendly and trotted towards me before scampering off,' he said.

On Saturday night Andrew Hazelhurst saw the cheeky Tamworths sneaking around Malmesbury. He was walking his dogs when the pigs appeared from behind a hedge. He later told reporters he was startled to see them in a built-up area. However, no one asked his dogs for their opinion. Imagine the shock for them – out for a peaceful walk, ready to water a few trees when suddenly:

Doggy thoughts – *Woof . . . woof . . . woof . . . ggrrr . . . whine . . . woof . . . woof.*

Translation: *What on earth are they? Are we going to have to fight them? Let's get out of here!*

Information on the runaways was passed to the police, but at first they weren't interested. Wiltshire police spokesman Peter Bull commented: 'They are no danger to the public and as long as they are not doing harm to people's property there is no need for us to go looking for them.'

(Yes, he really was called Bull. Yes, isn't that lucky in an animal story. No, I wouldn't tell you a porky.)

As the evidence came together it was clear the

pigs had a favourite hideout, a thicket near Tetbury Hill. It was perfect. The Tamworths had a clear view of anyone trying to sneak up on them and the densely packed trees and shrubs gave plenty of shelter from the weather. Even better, there was an old apple tree with plenty of windfalls lying on the ground. The fallen fruit added juicy morsels to their diet of roots and

worms. The owner of the thicket, Carl Saddler, was quite relaxed about the pigs – in fact, he thought they might do him a favour.

'They are welcome to stay as long as they want,' he said, 'and I'd be happy for them to dig out some of this undergrowth.'

Yet as the Tamworths enjoyed their new-found freedom they had no idea they were about to become stars. News of their getaway had seeped out of sleepy Malmesbury and caught the attention of journalists around the world.

## Tamworth Two Hold the Hearts of the Nation

When you think of newspapers and TV have you ever heard the phrase 'the silly season'? The silly season usually happens during the summer holiday, when there isn't any big news and the media spend a lot of time reporting small, oddball incidents. You know the kind of thing:

Loch Ness Monster spotted in Blackpool. 'It was wearing a bikini,' says eyewitness.

One in ten British school children are little, green aliens, confirms school survey.

Well, in 1998, the silly season came early. The media poured into Malmesbury in a blaze of initials – BBC, ITN, HTV, NBC, CNN, SKY. For four days the town was like Hollywood on Oscar night. And the first question the pressmen and TV crews asked was 'What are the pigs called?'

The brave Tamworths had already been given nicknames by the locals. Joan Richardson, an English literature professor, said, 'We call them Fred and Ginger because they had to perform some pretty fancy footwork to have escaped the butcher's knife.'

Fred and Ginger . . . fancy footwork . . . get the joke??? What, you don't know who she was talking about? Shame on you! Fred Astaire and Ginger Rogers were brilliant dancers in 1930s musicals. Don't you ever watch old black and white films on TV on wet Sunday afternoons. No? Boring?? What have pigs got to do with dancers???

Well, funny you should say that, because the reporters thought the same.

'We need catchy names,' they said.

'We need exciting names,' they said.

'Let's make them up,' they said.

So the pigs hit the headlines as the Tamworth Two or more intimately, Butch and Sundance. Butch Cassidy and the Sundance Kid were famous outlaws in the American West. Robert Redford and Paul Newman played them in one

of the best ever cowboy movies. In real life and in the film Butch and Sundance pulled off some amazing escapes. There was only one problem with giving these chunky names to the Tamworths — the sow had been called Butch.

The reporters soon found that Malmesbury residents held different points of view on the pig breakout. Roy Waine was horrified. He owned nearby fields and the pigs were making a mess of them by digging holes with their snuffling noses.

Roy fussed, 'They can't just be left to go around causing damage like this. I suppose they will have to be shot if they can't be caught alive. It sounds cruel but it's far better then letting them starve to death. Once the apples have run out, they are going to get very hungry if the ground freezes again.'

Damage? Shot? Starve? That wasn't what the news hounds wanted to hear. They knew that Britain was a nation of animal lovers and that cuddly animal stories sell papers. They wanted to report happy comments. Betty Ross, 75, gave them what they were looking for. 'I'd like to say,' said Betty, 'Go for it, pigs!'

## The Net Closes in on the Tamworth Two

By Thursday, January 15 the Tamworth Two were making headlines:

*Guardian*: **PLUCKY PORKERS RUN FOR THEIR LIVES**

*Times*: **BOARS ON THE RUN**

*Independent*: **THE PIGS THAT REALLY FLEW**

*Chicago Tribune*: **DUO FLEEING FOR THEIR LIVES HOG THE SPOTLIGHT**

And as the news broke dozens of well-wishers called Newman's. Peter was flabbergasted.

'I just couldn't believe the reaction,' he said. 'I had calls from all over the country, including one from a girls' boarding school in London that wants them. Unfortunately they are not mine, or they would be welcome to them.'

I'm sure the girls' school meant well – but don't you get this niggling feeling:

Headmistress to Cook: 'Cook, dear, I've just had this wonderful idea for cutting next term's meat bills. We rescue these pigs and in six months' time when everyone has forgotten about them . . .'

Arnaldo Dijulio, however, was still the owner of the pigs. At first he had been annoyed by the commotion over the Tamworths and insisted they had to be caught and taken back to the slaughterhouse. Then he thought again and realized that Christmas might come very early for him in 1998.

It dawned on Arnaldo that Butch and Sundance had done him an enormous favour. Dead they were only worth about £40 each, and he would be the blackest villain in Britain — Arnaldo the pig murderer! Yet now they were celebrities his Tamworths could fetch much more.

'If somebody makes an offer to me,' he said, 'they can take them off my hands.'

Across Fleet Street the cry went out, 'Grab the pigs'. The *Daily Express* offered Arnaldo £1000, but this was chicken feed. The *Daily Mail* swept all other paltry offers aside and fixed the deal for £15,000. But first the Tamworth Two had to be rounded up — and they weren't co-operating.

At each new sighting of the porky pair, crowds of journalists trampled across fields and gardens and ITN even had a helicopter out pig-spotting. A posse of seven *Daily Mail* reporters promised to save the pigs for the nation. Faced with this hubbub the Wiltshire police decided that Butch and Sundance had to be recaptured. Under mounting pressure the RSPCA were called in.

In the end Butch came easily. On Thursday evening she was cornered in a garden and whisked away to a secret retreat by the *Daily Mail*. Sundance, perhaps sensing that the honour of the Tamworths now fell on his shoulders, put up far more of a fight. Late that afternoon, he too was spotted rooting in a garden but he had chosen carefully. It was a huge two-acre open space near his hideaway.

For four long hours three policemen and an RSPCA inspector, armed with nets, ropes and lamps, chased Sundance in vain. Dodging, charging and barging he stayed stubbornly free. And when force failed, trickery was tried. Dave Lang, a nearby pig breeder, brought along Samantha, a well-built Tamworth sow to lure him out. Sundance caught her scent but was unimpressed – perhaps his heart was set on Butch alone. Whatever, shortly after 8 pm Sundance made his break and fled back to his hideout in the thicket. Wearily, the forces of law and order called a halt to the hunt.

## The Tamworth One . . .
## Sundance Alone

On Saturday 17 January, the odds mounted against Sundance. The police were back with tracker dogs and a trained marksman armed with a tranquillizer gun. Phil Buffy of the RSPCA said, 'The pig has suffered enough and this is the best way of safely capturing him.'

If Sundance was peering out of his thicket at around 1pm he could not have been blamed for thinking the RSPCA were talking nonsense. The tracker dogs — Pepsi, a spaniel and Barney, a lurcher — led a new assault on his liberty. But it wasn't the dogs that were likely to worry him — it was their owners. Pepsi and Barney belonged to two butchers from Stroud and the men had turned up in their shop clothes — striped overalls.

Really, if you were a fugitive pig, and your partner had already been caught, would you give yourself up to a posse that included two butchers? And what did the butchers have in mind? Did they believe their meat-chopping clothes were the only thing to wear when approaching pork . . . oops, sorry, a pig? Not surprisingly, Sundance was in no mood to surrender. The gallant Tamworth gave the dogs the run-around for over an hour . . . then his luck ran out.

Perhaps tired and confused by the barking dogs, Sundance made a mistake. Leaving the cover of the thicket, he made a break across an open field and sped straight into the sights of the RSPCA marksman. Even then the tough Tamworth gave his pursuers a shock as two tranquillizer darts bounced off his ginger hide. But the third shot hit home and he began to slow down. Seizing their chance, the men put a 'snout grabber' over his head (a kind of muzzle) and pulled him to the ground. His nine days of freedom and fame were over.

Two days later Butch and Sundance were reunited at an animal refugee centre. Since then they have lived like pigs in clover, as the stars of an education centre, showing how clever porkers can be. But when they are surrounded by adoring children do they dream of their days of wild adventure?

OK, it's a corny idea to finish the story with. But it might be true. Professor Stanley Curtis, of Pennsylvania State University, believes pigs are so bright that he has adapted computer games for them to play. He thinks they are able to have wishes and dreams and during 1998 was conducting experiments to find out about how pigs think. 'We want to know,' he said, 'if we keep a pig in a confined environment whether it is capable of wanting to be somewhere else. We want to know whether a pig that has seen an animal wallow in the mud begins to daydream about wallowing in the mud itself.'

So who knows? Butch and Sundance might really dream about their days of freedom. And perhaps about their companion who didn't get away.

# *Amazing Animals: Animals to the Rescue*

Peter Hepplewhite and Neil Tonge

Animals to the Rescue is packed with amazing true stories about animal bravery . . .

- In the 19th century a goose saved an entire British regiment from slaughter.

- The German police force recently brought in an undercover pig called Luise to bust a gang of drug dealers.

- In Canada a cougar saved a boy from freezing to death.

- In Jersey a giant gorilla cradled a toddler who fell into his enclosure until help arrived.

And that's just for starters . . .

# A selected list of titles available from Macmillan Children's Books

The prices shown below are correct at the time of going to press. However, Macmillan Publishers reserve the right to show new retail prices on covers which may differ from those previously advertised.